YASMIN

The Superhero

written by
SAADIA FARUQI

illustrated by
HATEM ALY

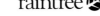
raintree
a Capstone company — publishers for children

To Mariam for inspiring me, and Mubashir for helping me find the right words—S.F.

To my sister, Eman, and her amazing girls, Jana and Kenzi—H.A.

Raintree is an imprint of Capstone Global Library Limited, a company incorporated in England and Wales having its registered office at 264 Banbury Road, Oxford, OX2 7DY – Registered company number: 6695582

www.raintree.co.uk
myorders@raintree.co.uk

Text © Capstone Global Library Limited 2020
The moral rights of the proprietor have been asserted.

Edited by Kristen Mohn
Designed by Lori Bye
Original illustrations © Capstone Global Library Limited 2020
Originated by Capstone Global Library Ltd
Printed and bound in India

ISBN 978 1 4747 6972 3
23 22 21 20
10 9 8 7 6 5 4 3 2

British Library Cataloguing in Publication Data
A full catalogue record for this book is available from the British Library.

Acknowledgements
Design Elements: Shutterstock: Art and Fashion, rangsan paidaenw

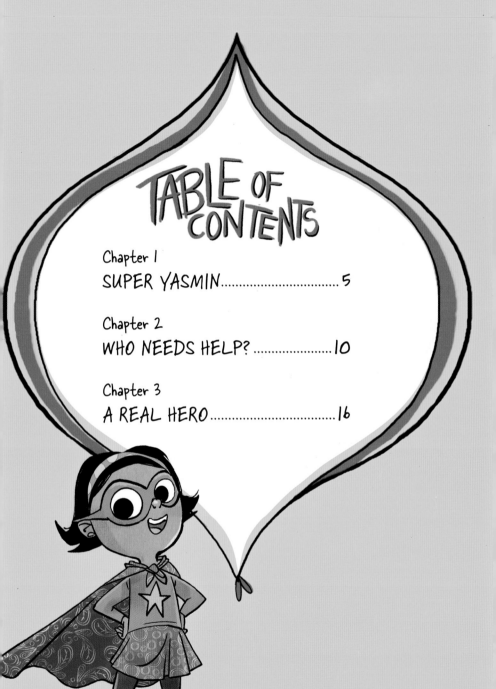

TABLE OF CONTENTS

CHAPTER 1

Super Yasmin

Yasmin loved reading with Baba. Her favourite stories were about superheroes.

Baba closed the book.

"I wish I was a superhero," Yasmin said.

"What do you like about superheroes?" Baba asked.

Yasmin thought. "Well, they save people," she said.

"From what?" asked Mama.

"From evil villains, of course!"
Yasmin said.

Mama laughed. "Enough
reading," she said. "The weather
is perfect. Why don't you go
outside and play?"

Yasmin skipped to Nana and Nani's room. "I'm Super Yasmin!" she announced. "I'm going outside to defeat evil villains!"

"That sounds like important work," Nani said. "But every superhero needs a costume."

Nani took her dupatta and draped it over Yasmin's shoulders. "Here is your cape."

Nana brought out his old sleeping mask. He cut two holes for Yasmin's eyes.

"Now you look just like a superhero," Nana said.

"Thanks!" Yasmin waved.

"I'm off to save the world!"

CHAPTER 2

Who needs help?

Yasmin went outside. Lots of children were playing. Some were cycling. Some kicked a football.

Yasmin searched everywhere. She couldn't see any evil villains. What was the point of being a superhero if there were no villains to defeat?

"Hello, Yasmin!" It was
Emma's mum. She was taking
in shopping bags from her
car. Oops! A bag fell and the
shopping spilled onto the street.

Yasmin ran to pick up the shopping. "Here you go, Mrs Winters," she said.

"Oh, you saved the day, Yasmin!" Mrs Winters said. "Thank you so much."

Yasmin continued her search for villains. Maybe one was hiding behind this tree! Nope.

"Hey, Yasmin," Ali called from his doorstep. "This maths problem is really hard. Can you help me?"

Yasmin worked out the answer in a jiffy. "Four hundred and seventy-five," she told him.

"You're so good at maths, Yasmin," Ali said. "Thanks a million!"

Yasmin waved and kept walking. She needed to find a villain.

CHAPTER 3

A real hero

At the end of the street, a little girl was crying. Her ball was stuck on a roof. Yasmin looked around. A big stick lay on the ground.

"Don't worry," she told the little girl. "This will do the trick."

The girl was happy to get her ball back. "Thank you! Thank you!" She jumped up and down.

"You're welcome," said Yasmin.

Where are all the villains? she wondered.

Yasmin went home,

disappointed. Baba was waiting

for her with a glass of cool lassi.

"Super Yasmin is back!"

Baba said.

"I'm not a superhero," Yasmin mumbled. "I didn't find a single evil villain to defeat." She took a sip of her lassi and sighed.

Baba hugged her close. "I saw that you helped many people on our street today," he said. "That's what real superheroes do!"

"They do?" asked Yasmin.

"Of course! Evil villains are only in story books," Baba said. "In real life, superheroes are the ones who go out of their way to be kind and helpful."

Yasmin gulped down her lassi. "You're right. I did help!" she exclaimed. "I suppose I really am Super Yasmin!"

Baba laughed. "Come inside now," he said. "Even superheroes have to do their homework."

Think about it, talk about it

* Superheroes have special powers or abilities – and so do people! What do you think Yasmin's superpowers are? What are your superpowers?

* Make up a superhero of your own. Draw a picture and give him or her a name. What special skills does your superhero have? Is there a particular problem your superhero must solve?

* Think about someone you admire, someone who is super! What do you admire about this person? What special skill do they have that makes them a superhero?

Learn Urdu with Yasmin!

Yasmin's family speaks both English and Urdu. Urdu is a language from Pakistan. Perhaps you already know some Urdu words!

baba father

dupatta shawl or scarf

jaan life; a sweet nickname for a loved one

kameez long tunic or shirt

lassi yoghurt drink

nana grandfather on mother's side

nani grandmother on mother's side

salaam hello

shalwar loose trousers

shukriya thank you

Pakistan fun facts

Yasmin and her family are proud of their Pakistani culture. Yasmin loves to share facts about Pakistan!

Location

Pakistan is on the continent of Asia, with India on one side and Afghanistan on the other.

Islamabad

PAKISTAN

Founder

Muhammad Ali Jinnah was the founder of Pakistan.

Heroes

Abdul Sattar Edhi was a Pakistani humanitarian who created the world's largest volunteer ambulance network. He is considered a Pakistani hero.

Two people from Pakistan have won a Nobel Prize: Malala Yousafzai for Peace in 2014 and Abdus Salam for Physics in 1979.

Make a paper bag superhero!

YOU WILL NEED:

- small paper bag
- construction paper
- scissors
- felt-tips or crayons
- glue stick or tape
- pipe cleaners
- optional: glitter, wool (for hair), other craft supplies

STEPS:

1. Flatten the paper bag and put the bottom of the bag at the top. Draw eyes and a mouth on the folded part of the bag.

2. Cut a mask out of construction paper, or draw one on. Use construction paper to make a cape. Decorate the mask and cape with whatever patterns you choose. Glue them onto the paper bag to make the superhero's costume.

3. Glue or tape pipe cleaners to the sides of the bag for the superhero's arms.

4. Create a logo for the front of your superhero. Use your initial or draw a symbol. Use other craft supplies to add finishing touches to your superhero, and you've finished!

About the author

Saadia Faruqi is a Pakistani American writer, interfaith activist and cultural sensitivity trainer previously profiled in *O Magazine*. She is author of the adult short story collection, *Brick Walls: Tales of Hope & Courage from Pakistan*. Her essays have been published in *Huffington Post*, *Upworthy* and *NBC Asian America*. She lives in Texas, USA, with her husband and children.

Hatem Aly is an Egyptian-born illustrator whose work has been featured in multiple publications worldwide. He currently lives in New Brunswick, Canada, with his wife, son and more pets than people. When he is not dipping cookies in a cup of tea or staring at blank pieces of paper, he is usually drawing books. One of the books he illustrated is *The Inquisitor's Tale* by Adam Gidwitz, which won a Newbery Honour and other awards, despite Hatem's drawings of a farting dragon, a two-headed cat and stinky cheese.

Join Yasmin
on all her adventures!

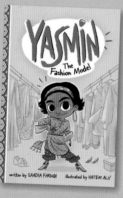

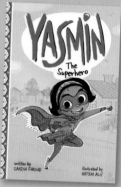

Discover more at

www.raintree.co.uk